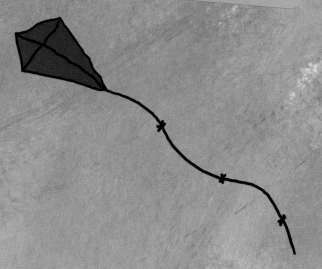

For Neal

Walter Was Worried

Laura Vaccaro Seeger

A Neal Porter Book
ROARING BROOK PRESS
New York

Walter was

worried

when

the sky grew

dark.

Priscilla was

pUZZLEd

when

the fog rolled

in.

Shirley was

SHOCKED

when

lightning lit the

sky.

Frederick was

FRIGHTENED

when

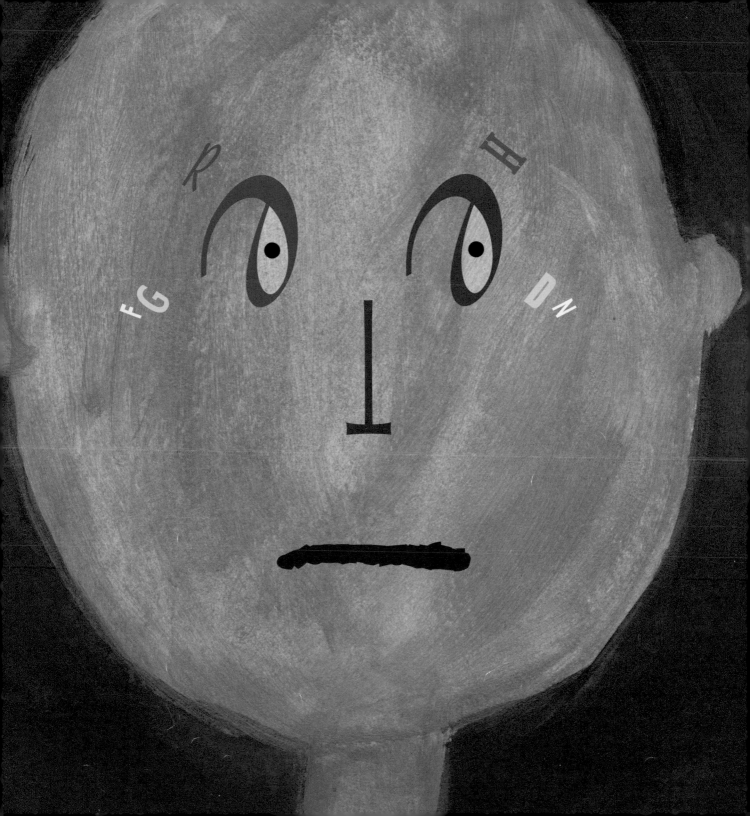

thunder shook the

trees.

Ursula was

when

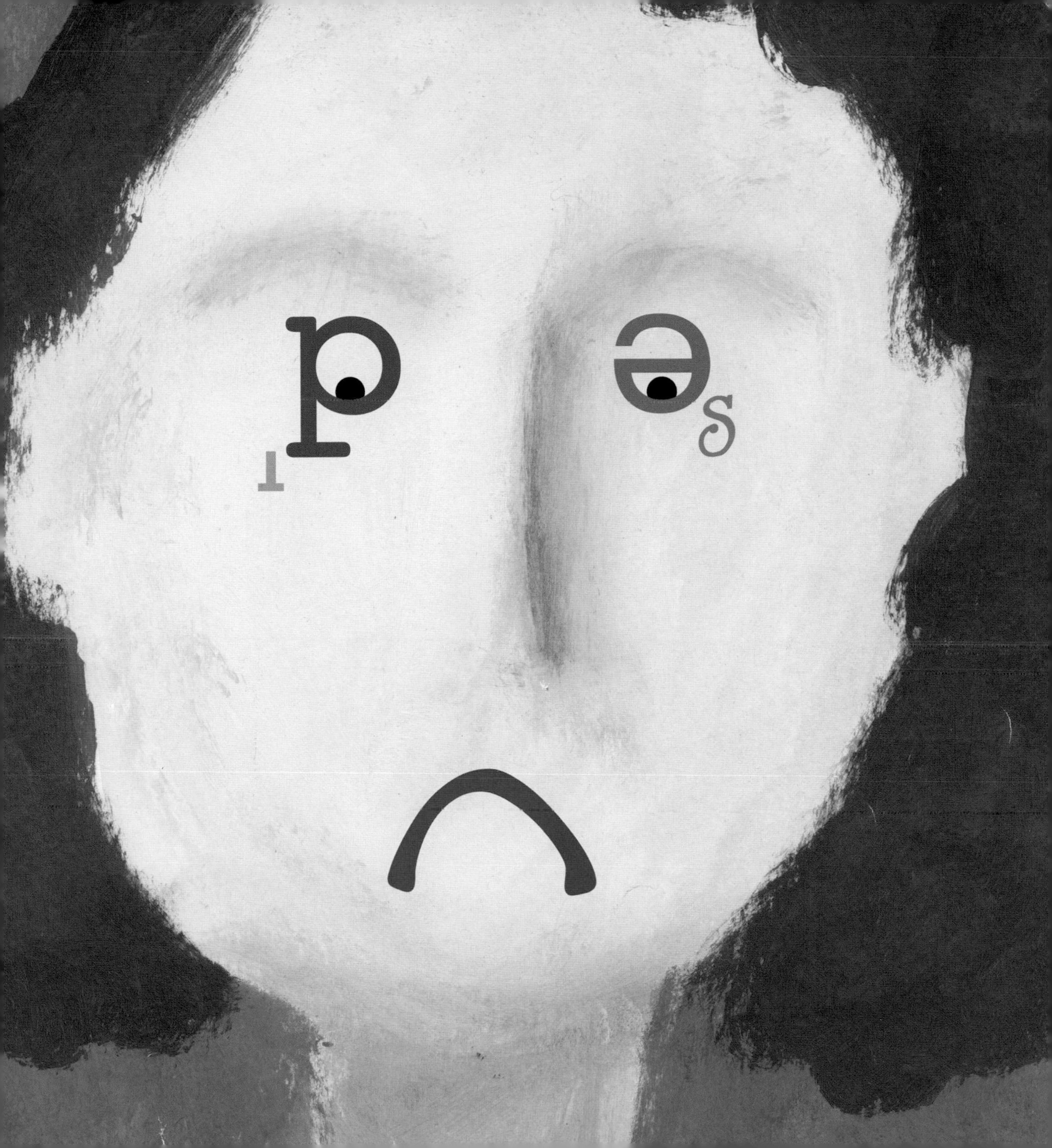

the rain came

down.

Then...

Delilah was

DELIGHTED

when

the rain turned to

snow.

Henry was

HOPEFUL

when

the sky began to

clear.

And...

Elliot was

ecstatic

when

the sun came

out.

Text and illustrations copyright © 2005 by Laura Vaccaro Seeger
A Neal Porter Book
Published by Roaring Brook Press
Roaring Brook Press is a division of Holtzbrinck Publishing Holdings Limited Partnership
175 Fifth Avenue, New York, New York 10010
mackids.com

Library of Congress Cataloging-in-Publication Data
Seeger, Laura Vaccaro.
Walter was worried / Laura Vaccaro Seeger.— 1st ed.
p. cm.
"A Neal Porter book."
Summary: Children's faces, depicted with letters of the alphabet, react to the onset of a storm
and its aftermath in this picture book, accompanied by simple alliterative text.
ISBN 978-1-59643-068-6
[1. Storms—Fiction.   2. Emotions—Fiction.   3. Alliteration.] I. Title.
PZ7.S4514Wal 2005   [E]—dc22   2004024558

New edition ISBN 978-1-62672-251-4

Our books may be purchased for promotional, educational,
or business use. Please contact your local bookseller or the Macmillan Corporate and Premium
Sales Department at (800) 221-7945 ext. 5442 or by e-mail at MacmillanSpecialMarkets@macmillan.com.

First edition 2005
New edition 2016
Printed in China by RR Donnelley Asia Printing Solutions Ltd., Dongguan City, Guangdong Province
10 9 8 7 6 5 4 3 2 1